That's the Spirit, Claude

Story by Joan Lowery Nixon
Pictures by Tracey Campbell Pearson

Viking

VIKING
Published by the Penguin Group
Penguin Books USA Inc.,
375 Hudson Street, New York, New York 10014, U.S.A.
Penguin Books Ltd, 27 Wrights Lane, London W8 5TZ, England
Penguin Books Australia Ltd, Ringwood, Victoria, Australia
Penguin Books Canada Ltd, 10 Alcorn Avenue, Toronto, Ontario, Canada M4V 3B2
Penguin Books (N.Z.) Ltd, 182–190 Wairau Road, Auckland 10, New Zealand

Penguin Books Ltd, Registered Offices: Harmondsworth, Middlesex, England

First published in 1992 by Viking Penguin, a division of Penguin Books USA Inc.

3   5   7   9   10   8   6   4   2

Library of Congress Cataloging-in-Publication Data
Nixon, Joan Lowery. That's the spirit, Claude / by Joan Lowery Nixon; illustrated by
Tracey Campbell Pearson.   p. cm.   Summary: When Shirley convinces her husband
Claude to help fulfill their adopted daughter's dream of a visit from Santa, she doesn't
reckon on the real Santa Claus showing up at their place in Texas.
ISBN 0-670-83434-3
[1. Santa Claus—Fiction.   2. Christmas—Fiction.
3. Frontier and pioneer life—Fiction.   4. Humorous stories.]
I. Pearson, Tracey Campbell, ill.   II. Title.
PZ7.N65Tk 1992 [E]—dc20   91-47742   CIP   AC

Printed in Mexico
Set in Cheltenham Book

CHAPTER ONE

Days were growing shorter, golden leaves were falling, and there was a snap in the air loud enough to be heard clear down on the border. Inside a cosy cabin, deep within that great state called Texas, Shirley and Claude relaxed beside a crackling fire with their adopted young'uns, ten-year-old Tom and his eight-year-old sister, Deputy Sheriff Bessie.

Shirley put down her sewing and turned to Bessie. "Whatever you're knittin' is twice as long as you are and near wide enough to fit around Claude. What is it?" she asked.

"It's my Christmas stockin'," Bessie said. She stood on a chair and held it up high.

Claude smiled at Bessie. "I give you credit for bein' a good deputy sheriff and keepin' wrong-minded folks away from our farm," he said. "But, daughter, I think you got a misconception about size. You're gonna get lost inside that stockin'."

"It's not for me to wear," Bessie said, shaking her head so hard her curls bounced like pork fat on a hot griddle. "This is the stockin' I'm gonna put out for Sandy Claus."

"Who's Sandy Claus?" Shirley asked.

"You never heard of Sandy Claus?" Bessie took a deep breath. "It's a long story, but I'll tell you all about him."

Claude interrupted. He knew about Bessie's long stories. "No thanks," he said. "I already know all I'll ever want to know about a man with a foot and leg big enough to fit that stockin'. I just hope I never meet up with him."

Tom laughed. "Bessie's knittin' that stockin' to hold the goodies she's hopin' to get on Christmas Day. Sandy Claus isn't big. He's short, with a rosy face and a beard that's as white as the snow. And he's got a little round belly that shakes when he laughs like a bowl full of strawberry preserves."

Bessie jumped from her chair and laid down her stocking and knitting needles. "That's right! And every Christmas Eve, Sandy Claus puts on a red suit and hat and fills his sleigh with toys and candy."

Tom interrupted: "Then he hitches up eight tiny reindeer and flies all around the world landin' on roofs, and jumpin' down chimneys, and leavin' goodies for boys and girls in their stockin's which was hung by their chimneys with care. And all the time he's doin' that, he keeps sayin' 'Ho, ho, ho.'"

Claude frowned. "If that Sandy Claus feller is braggin' on hisself with a wild story like that, I'm guessin' that when he went down the first chimney he landed on his head."

Bessie's eyes filled with tears. "Sandy Claus is tellin' the truth," she said. "He never came to our house, but our ma said he would someday, and she told the truth, too. She even read us a poem a man writ about him, only the man didn't know Sandy Claus's real name, so he called him St. Nick."

"Well, maybe Sandy Claus rides on his sleigh to some parts of the world," Claude admitted, "but, far as I ever heard tell, he's never made his way to Texas. You'll be a lot happier, daughter, if you just put Sandy Claus out of your mind."

Tom looked disappointed, but he tried to smile at Bessie. "Don't be sad, Bessie," he said bravely. "On Christmas we'll go into town to church, and we'll sing Christmas songs, and I'll bake a Christmas pudding. We don't need Sandy Claus."

Well, Shirley never could abide to disappoint a child, so she began to think on a way to make Bessie's and Tom's wishes come true.

And, while she was deep in thought, Claude said, "Tell you what, young'uns. Come Christmastime, I'll cut us down a nice little pine tree, and you can make paper stars to hang on it."

Shirley smiled.

"That's the spirit, Claude," she said.

CHAPTER TWO

Bessie went back to her knitting, and after a while she said, "I been thinkin'. Maybe Sandy Claus never came to Texas because he never got an invite. I'm gonna write him a letter and tell him where we live."

"How will you know where to send the letter?" Shirley asked.

"Ma told us Sandy Claus lives at the North Pole," Tom said.

"Where's that?" Shirley asked.

"All I know is it's north of Texas," Tom answered.

"Iffen it's that far off, then Bessie'd better get to writin' her letter," Shirley suggested. "She can mail it when we go into town tomorrow."

Bessie grinned. "I know that Sandy Claus will be real pleased with my invite and come. On Christmas Eve, I'm gonna hang up my stockin' right here by the fire so it'll be ready for him."

Later, after Bessie and Tom had been tucked into bed, Claude shook his head and said, "Shirley, I'm sorely afeard those young'uns are in for a heap of disappointment. No matter how I figger it, there's no way that feller who jumps down chimneys is gonna have time to get to all the houses between the North Pole and Texas."

Shirley nodded agreement, but she answered, "I been givin' this a heap of thought, Claude. From what the young'uns told us, Sandy Claus 'pears to look a lot like you." Quickly she added, "Same handsome figger of a man, I mean."

"What are you gettin' at?" Claude asked.

"You and I already started makin' a few toys and play pretties, like the rag doll for Bessie and the top for Tom. On Christmas Eve I could wrap up some molasses taffy chews, and we could add an apple and some pecan nuts and put all the toys and goodies in their stockin's, if that's where they want 'em."

"Fine with me," Claude said.

"Then all we'll need is Sandy Claus to make the young'uns happy," Shirley said. "Since the real Sandy Claus isn't likely to be on hand, that's where you come in."

"Now just a goldarned minute!" Claude said.

Shirley went on. "You can wear your red flannel nightcap and your red long johns and put flour on your beard to make it white. Then you can fill the stockin's and say, 'Ho, ho, ho.'"

"That's a fool idea!" Claude said. "I'm not gonna do it."

Well, Shirley never could abide to disappoint a child, so she said, "The children's ma made 'em a promise, Claude. I think we should keep it."

Claude thought on it a moment. Then he said, "Even iffen I do agree to be Sandy Claus, I *won't* come down the dadblamed chimney!"

"Never expected you to," Shirley said.

"All right, then," Claude mumbled. "I'll be the young'uns' Sandy Claus."

Shirley's smile was as sweet as honey oozin' from a hive.

"That's the spirit, Claude!" she said.

CHAPTER THREE

On Christmas Eve, Bessie proudly hung her stocking next to Tom's stocking. Tom's hung nicely at the side of the fireplace, but Bessie's stocking trailed down the wall and onto the floor.

"Do you think Sandy Claus will really come?" Bessie asked Shirley for the umpteenth time.

Shirley winked at Claude and said, "I wouldn't be a bit surprised."

"Tom and me aim to sneak out of our beds when we hear his reindeer on the roof," Bessie said. "Then, when Sandy Claus is puttin' goodies in our stockin's we'll get a look at him."

"Let's go to bed now," Tom said to Bessie. "The sooner we're in bed, the sooner he might come."

The minute Tom and Bessie were out of sight, Shirley whispered to Claude, "I forgot about the reindeer. It's lucky Bessie reminded me. Afore you come in the door, get up on the roof and make the kind of noise reindeer would make."

Claude scowled. "How am I supposed to know a fool thing like that?"

"You can figger it out," Shirley said. She pulled him outside. "Here's a sack with the goodies in it, here's your flannel night-cap, and here's some flour for your beard. Get down to your long johns. You can leave your clothes on the stoop."

Claude did as she said, but since he was wearing only his red long johns, boots, and nightcap, he shivered. "It's cold out here," he complained.

"I'm beholden to you, Claude," Shirley said and kissed him. "Quick. Make a noise on the roof, then come inside."

Claude hauled a ladder out of the barn, raised it to the roof, and began to climb it, grumbling to himself. "Make a noise. Make a noise. What kind of a noise?"

Well, Claude didn't need to fret himself about what kind of noise to make, because just as he hoisted himself onto the roof he heard such a rattling, ringing, and scraping going on beside him that he let out a yell. Someone else yelled, too, and crashed smack into Claude, and the two of them rolled off the roof and landed *thump* on the ground.

"By golly, that smarts!" a voice said.

Claude looked up to see a short man in a red suit with a rosy face and a white beard. The man rubbed his backside and scowled at Claude. "If that don't beat all," he said. "Here's another old coot pretendin' to be me! And you're the sorriest-lookin' imitation Sandy Claus I ever seen!"

Claude stared in surprise. "You're Sandy Claus?" he asked. "We wasn't expectin' you to come all the way to Texas."

"Don't know why not," Sandy Claus said. "I got a letter from a Deputy Sheriff Bessie tellin' me to come, so I came." Sandy Claus placed a finger longside of his nose and gave a wise nod. "I never mess with the law," he said.

Claude scrambled up and quickly pulled on his clothes. "Welcome to Texas," he said. "Can't recollect when I've ever been so glad to see anybody."

Claude helped Sandy Claus get to his feet and shoved the bag of goodies at him. "This is for the young'uns," Claude said. "They been waitin' for you. Come on inside."

"I'm fixin' to. Don't rush me," Sandy Claus grumbled. But he took hold of the bag, and Claude saw that Sandy Claus had his own bundle of toys neatly flung on his back.

Claude threw open the front door, then paused to look up at the roof. Consarned if there really wasn't a team of reindeer up there, each one prancin' and pawin' with each tiny hoof.

"That's not gonna help the dadblamed roof any," Claude muttered.

He followed Sandy Claus, who stomped into the house shouting, "Ho, ho, ho."

Shirley stared at Sandy Claus and gasped, and Claude could hear other gasps behind the partly open door to the young'uns' bedroom.

"Shirley," Claude said, remembering his manners, "this here's Sandy Claus."

Shirley collected herself enough to say, "Howdy, Sandy. We're glad you came. Set yourself down and stay a spell."

"Pleased to make your acquaintance, ma'am," Sandy Claus said, "but I cain't stay. I got work to do. Any stockin's here that need to be filled with goodies?"

As he turned toward the fireplace his eyes opened wide, and he staggered back. "Whose is *that*?" he asked, pointing at Bessie's Christmas stocking.

"Deputy Sheriff Bessie's," Claude answered.

Sandy Claus wiped his forehead. "Hoo boy! That's a powerful big deputy to keep happy," he said. "I better get to work."

Saying, "Ho, ho, ho," he put toys and goodies in Tom's and Bessie's stockings, then fished through his pockets and pulled out a letter.

"Deputy Sheriff Bessie done give me the names of a few other young'uns who live nearby," Sandy Claus said to Claude. "How about if I leave their toys and goodies with you folks, and you deliver 'em for me in the mornin'? That welcome I got on your rooftop not only throwed me off schedule, but I'd like to avoid gettin' another one like it."

Well, Shirley never could abide to disappoint a child, so she said, "We'll deliver 'em right now, afore the kiddies wake up."

But Claude looked Sandy Claus firmly in the eye and said, "We'll do it only iffen you promise to keep comin' back each year to Texas."

Sandy Claus scowled and said, "I'll come back only iffen you promise to stop runnin' around your roof in your long johns!"

"Done," Claude said.

They had no sooner shook hands on it, when Sandy Claus hightailed it out the door.

Shirley and Claude heard him exclaim afore he drove out of sight, "Merry Christmas to all, and good night nellie! I wonder how many more sorry-lookin' pretend Sandy Clauses I'm gonna run into tonight!"

"Bessie! Tom!" Claude shouted. "Bundle up warm while I hitch up the horses to the wagon. We're goin' to help out Sandy Claus and deliver some gifts."

Shirley's smile was so bright it lit the room like the sun at high noon, and she gave Claude a hug that had all the warmth and love of Christmas in it.

"That's the spirit, Claude!" she said.